MW00906262

The Little Alvernon Stories
Volume 1

Linda Lee Boynton Pedersen

Illustrated by

Larry Vernon Boynton

Linda Boynton Pedersen

Copyright 2013 © Linda Boynton Pedersen

ISBN-13: 978-1492868477

DEDICATION

To the grown up Little Alvernon
who was my father

Nancy,
May these stories
bring joy and laughter
to your life as they have to mine.
God bless
Linda Boynton Pedersen
2013

Gracious words are a honeycomb,
sweet to the soul
and healing to the bones.
Proverbs 16.24

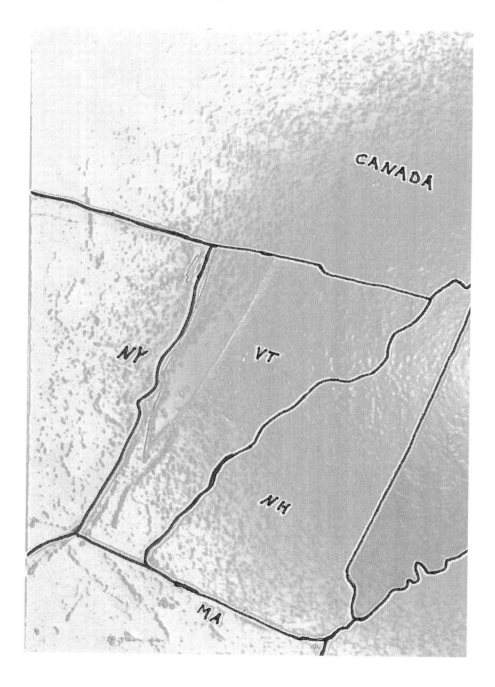

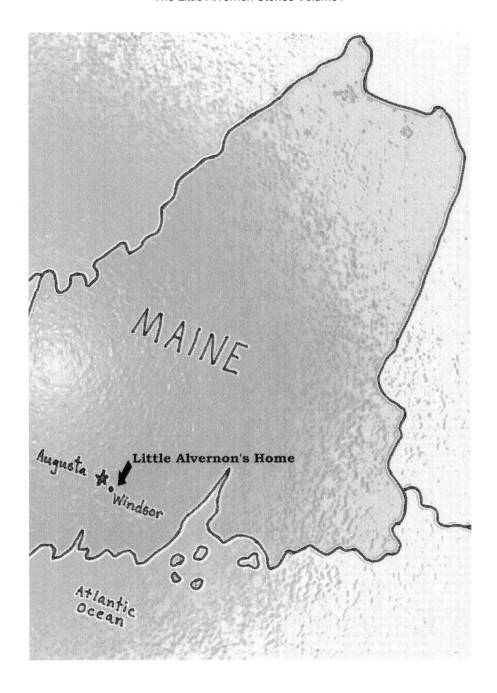

Little Alvernon's House

At the Crossroads

Tyler's Corner

Windsor, Maine

The Little Alvernon Stories Volume 1

TABLE OF CONTENTS

ACKNOWLEDGEMENTS

It is with heart-felt gratitude that I acknowledge the help of my whole family in completing this first volume of The Little Alvernon Stories:

To my father who wrote down in his own hand the first written drafts of the Little Alvernon stories before he died;

To my mother who was my father's secretary, editor, and sounding board;

To my brother Larry who created in his unique style the original full-color illustration for the cover and many black and white images for the stories before losing his battle with cancer;

To my sisters Connie and Joyce who have shared their knowledge of family history with love and laughter and a deep sense of pride and joy;

To my husband Bob who has continued to prod and encourage me to "get those stories published;"

To all my children and grandchildren who have inspired me to share these precious memories of their grandfather [great grandfather].

Boynton Pedersen

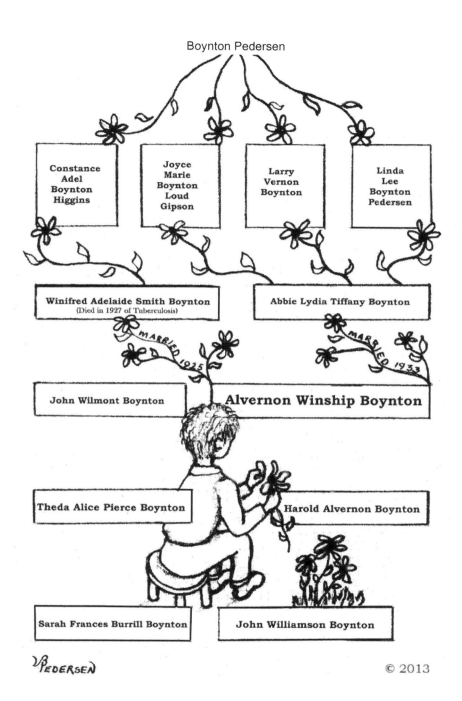

Constance Adel Boynton Higgins

Joyce Marie Boynton Loud Gipson

Larry Vernon Boynton

Linda Lee Boynton Pedersen

Winifred Adelaide Smith Boynton
(Died in 1927 of Tuberculosis)

Abbie Lydia Tiffany Boynton

MARRIED 1925

MARRIED 1933

John Wilmont Boynton

Alvernon Winship Boynton

Theda Alice Pierce Boynton

Harold Alvernon Boynton

Sarah Frances Burrill Boynton

John Williamson Boynton

𝒱ᴘᴇᴅᴇʀѕᴇɴ

© 2013

Prologue

These stories are about a little boy growing up on a farm in Maine as told by the same boy when he was grown up. They happened about a hundred years ago. This boy's name was Little Alvernon. This is an unusual and old-fashioned name. Perhaps you have never heard it. Do you know how to pronounce it? You must put the emphasis on the middle sound – the **VER** to say it correctly: Al-**ver**-non.

As you read these stories, you will find that Little Al**ver**non loved to have fun, but sometimes he got himself into predicaments. Did you ever find yourself in a *predicament*? I hesitate to use this expression because it is such a long word. However, perhaps telling you about Little Alvernon's father will help to explain its meaning.

His name was Harold Alvernon, and at the time he was being born, he was in a special kind of predicament. You see, he had a hard time coming into the world because he was not in the usual position for babies to be born. Finally, when he did make it, he could not breathe. Fortunately, an old granny nurse who was standing by used every skill she knew to save his life. Nothing seemed to work. Until, at last, she picked him up in her arms, put her mouth to his, and breathed the breath of life into his tiny form. What a happy sound was that baby's first cry! The old granny nurse, whose name I do not know, was rewarded for her efforts and tender loving care.

When Harold Alvernon's father and mother discovered that he had been born on April Fool's Day, they immediately wondered if this might be the beginning of a birthday predicament for the rest of his life. They thought about the possibility of people chanting "APRIL FOOL" instead of "HAPPY BIRTHDAY" every time he had a birthday cake.

So, they decided to declare his birthday to be April 2, when he really entered the world a few minutes before midnight on April 1. But it was not really very far from the truth, nor was it totally wrong, for he did not breathe his first breath until after midnight on April 2, 1879.

It is very interesting to see how much it cost Harold Alvernon to be born. Look at the copy of the real bill that Dr. Nelson sent to John and Sarah Frances for eight house calls during the birthing time. Isn't the sum of 75 cents a visit incredible?

A few years later, when this same little boy, Harold Alvernon, was in grammar school, he learned a poem entitled "The Curious Puppy," which on occasion he was called upon to recite to any listening audience. You will notice that this favorite poem of Harold Alvernon also talks about a predicament, but here it is called a *scrape*.

The Curious Puppy

There was once a little puppy
That was curiously inclined.
He nosed about and nosed about
To see what he could find.

One day upon an ash heap
An old teapot he spied
Forthwith he poked his nose in
To see what was inside.

The puppy's ears were very large
And the teapot's mouth was small,
So when he tried to pull his head out,
It wouldn't come at all.

The puppy barked and whined and howled
And kept up such a clatter,
John and Marion running came
To see what was the matter!

John took the puppy in his arms
And tried to keep him still,
While Marion seized the teapot
And they both pulled with a will.

But all their efforts were in vain.
His dogship found out then
It was easier to get in a scrape
Than to get out again.

"We'll take him to a tin man,"
Then Master Johnnie cried.
So dog and teapot in his arms
Down the long street they hied.

The tin man quickly plied his shears
And set the puppy free,
And the way he ran back up the street
It was a sight to see.

And now when ere his dogship
A curious thing he spies
He pokes his nose in as before
But keeps his ears outside!
                    (Anonymous)

I am sure Little Alvernon heard this poem recited many times by his father, Harold Alvernon, and perhaps was reminded of it when he, in turn, found himself in a *scrape* or *predicament.*

AUTHOR'S NOTE

To set the stage, each of the Little Alvernon Stories began with...

"Once upon a time there was a little boy named Little Alvernon. He had big brown eyes and beautiful dark wavy hair. He lived with his mother and father and younger brother in a farmhouse at the crossroads in the country."

You the reader may wish to carry on this tradition by repeating this introduction before each story.

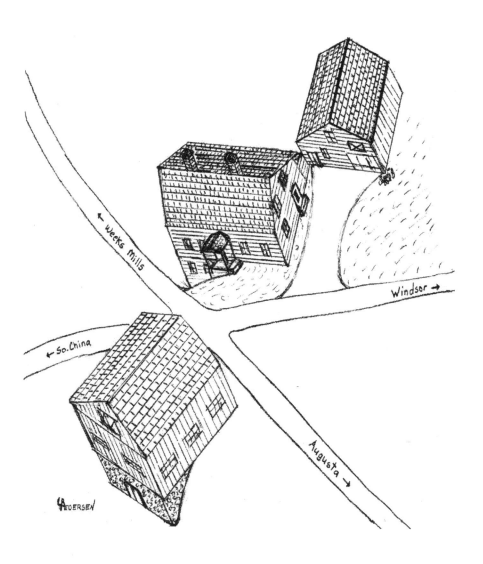

The Little Alvernon Stories Volume 1

The Crossroads

A crossroad happens when four roads come together and cross each other. Little Alvernon was proud that he could tell anyone who asked where each of the roads went. The road right in front of his house went up the hill to the church, the graveyard, his school, and eventually to the Windsor Fairgrounds.

If you followed the road the other way, it would take you to China (Maine, that is) where the telephone operator lived. He had visited there a few times and tried to figure out how the switchboard worked with all the wires, plugs, and holes with numbers. He knew that the telephone operator wearing her headphones was the one who connected the people who wanted to talk, but the rest was a wondrous mystery.

The road across from his house that ran in front of the cow barn was the one to take to go to Augusta, the big city. He knew it was ten miles away because he had heard his Ma and Pa say so. That road going the other way was where most of his neighbors lived. (It eventually took you to Weeks Mills.)

There were about a dozen houses at the crossroads and each one had extra land at some other location to support at least one cow. Little Alvernon's father had two tracts of land that could support as many as ten cows, a pair of workhorses, and sometimes a good driving horse. (A good driving horse pulling a carriage could go to the city in about an hour.)

You must remember that these roads were quite different. They were just plain dirt. When the weather was wet, the roads were muddy. When there was a hot, dry spell, the roads were powdery and deliciously warm - perfect for bare feet.

It was on one of those perfect-for-bare-feet days in June that Little Alvernon's mother asked him to do her a favor. (And, of course, he said, "Yes.") She wanted him to take the Larkin Catalog* down to Aunt Hellie.

This was the beginning of one of Little Alvernon's predicaments.

*The Larkin Catalog was a publication of the Larkin Company which served as a mail-order supplier to the entire United States. The catalog featured soap, household goods, furniture, food, medicines, paint; in short, almost everything.

Aunt Hellie's Back Door

A unt Hellie and Uncle Gussie lived in the third house down from Little Alvernon's. Aunt Hellie was quite short and wide, while Uncle Gussie was very tall. He had a mustache and talked through his nose. They liked to argue and try different ways to get the better of one another.

For instance, one day, Uncle Gussie hired his grandson for a quarter to go down in the field and "turn the hay" so that it could be put into the barn that afternoon. The grandson knew how to take advantage of the situation. He went into the house and told his grandmother what he had been paid to do. Aunt Hellie gave him another quarter **not** to do the job. Then they did not see the grandson again for at least three days.

On his way to Aunt Hellie's, with the Larkin Catalog* tucked under his arm, Little Alvernon saw at once how he could do a favor for not only one person, but possibly for three people, in one trip:

1) Do the errand for his mother,
2) Deliver the catalog to Aunt Hellie, and
3) Get a piece of Aunt Hellie's vanilla cake for himself, which he knew would be three inches square and one and a half inches thick, with a quarter of an inch of white frosting on top.

As he scuffed along the soft, dusty road, he felt the warm, sun-dried dirt on his bare feet. Little puffs of dust came up between his toes like the smoke from a train chugging along a track.

The front side of Aunt Hellie's house, except for the door, was covered with a climbing vine. The front door was closed, so Little Alvernon decided to use the back door (which he often did).

It must be said here that Aunt Hellie was quite hard of hearing and talked to herself a lot. On this day, she was sitting in the parlor just inside the front door, but she could see the back door through the kitchen – if she should look that way.

When Little Alvernon reached the back door, the inside door was open, but the screen door was locked. This was the beginning of a predicament. He knocked politely, but got no response. He began pounding and pointing, and Aunt Hellie, who was still in the parlor, finally noticed the movements at the back door and said sweetly, "Lift the latch and come right in."

Now this was the second time that Little Alvernon was supposed to lift the latch and come in, and he had been unable to do it both times. When Aunt Hellie said, "Don't bother to knock, just come right in," Little Alvernon answered, "I can't. The door's locked."

This exchange went on for some time...

Aunt Hellie: "Come right in."

Little Alvernon (loudly): "I can't. The door's locked!"

Aunt Hellie: "Don't knock. Come right in."

Little Alvernon (louder): "I can't! The door's LOCKED!"

Aunt Hellie (still sweetly): "Come right in."

Little Alvernon (at the top of his lungs):

"I CAN'T! THE DOOR'S LOCKED!"

Finally, Aunt Hellie came out to the kitchen and looked at the locked screen door. Laughing, she said, "Mmm... I guess I locked that door, didn't I!"

She let Little Alvernon in and said, "Thank you," as he handed her the Larkin Catalog.

Aunt Hellie right away went to the cupboard and brought down the cake tin. "Would you like a piece of Aunt Hellie's cake?" Without waiting for an answer, she cut a piece of vanilla cake which was three inches square and one and a half inches thick, with a quarter of an inch of white frosting on top.

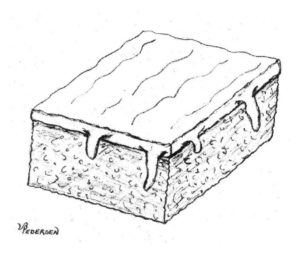

As Little Alvernon puffed his way homeward on the warm dirt road, he licked the last bit of the sweet frosting from his lips and thought how nice it was to do favors for people. Little did he know that the next set of predicaments in his life would be caused by his own mistakes concerning the farm animals.

Big Mistakes

The following account of events embarrassed Little Alvernon and he did not wish to talk about them. But the important details are set down here to be as fair as possible to all concerned: the pig, Uncle Gussie, Little Alvernon and his mother, father, grandmother, the calf, the squawking rooster, and his protective mother, the biddy hen.

The First Mistake

Now it so happened that Little Alvernon and his friend Alec chanced to be out looking at Uncle Gussie's pig. Uncle Gussie took great pride in his pig and kept the pen spotless and the pig nice and clean. Suddenly, Alec said, "Let's see if we can ride the pig."

Thinking about it afterwards, Little Alvernon wondered if Alec had tried this before and failed, but had worked out a good escape route by running down behind the barn, where he could hide but still see what was going on.

Alec took his turn first. As Alec chased the pig and tried to jump on its back, it "OOFED" and squealed a loud "EEEEEEE!" After a couple of tries and noisy results, Alec ran down behind the barn as fast as he could go.

Then Little Alvernon took his turn, and the pig "OOFED" and squealed "EEEEEEE" all the louder.

Vernon

By this time Uncle Gussie came out to see what the ruckus was all about. Right here is where Little Alvernon made his mistake.

When he saw Uncle Gussie, he should have followed Alec down behind the barn. But he panicked and started to crawl under the barbed wire fence. He knew instinctively, although he had never learned it in school, that a straight line is the shortest distance between two points. He was heading for Aunt Ida's backyard and the stable door – the shortest way home – which is where he wanted to be right then. Uncle Gussie did not have to catch Little Alvernon; the barbed wire did – AND tore a hole in the seat of his pants.

Later, when Uncle Gussie, in his usual high nasal twang, told Little Alvernon's father what he had done, Little Alvernon's father said, "I'll take care of it, Gus."

And he did.

Not long after his episode with the pig, Little Alvernon had an overwhelming desire to make up for the trouble he had caused, especially for the tear in the seat of his pants. So he found a grain bag, took his mother's scissors, a spool of black thread, and a needle, and went out to the stable. He cut the bottom off the grain bag. Then he cut up the middle for the two legs. He threaded the needle and, using double thread, sewed up the two inside seams.

By punching holes around the top, he was able to thread a piece of rope through for a belt. These crazy pants came just below his knees. Now-a-days, Little Alvernon's creation might be right in style.

The Second Mistake

Another day, Little Alvernon was in the "tie-up," the stalls where the cows were tied up, fed, and milked. He was there to clean out the manure while the cows were out in the pasture, so the floor would be clean and dry before the cows came home at night.

The only animal in sight was a frisky calf tied to the wall by a strong chain. The calf's big brown eyes watched Little Alvernon as he did his chore.

Little Alvernon stopped working and went over to pat the calf. "Hmmm," he said to himself, as he rubbed the calf's ear, "Just my size. Wouldn't it be fun to ride him?"

And so, forgetting his first mistake with Uncle Gussie's pig, he made his second big mistake. He tried to jump onto the calf's back.

He got his body across, but before he could get his leg over, the calf bucked and jumped sideways. With an OOF and a SPLAT, Little Alvernon landed flat on his back in the stinking, slippery manure trough of the cow stalls. He had to roll over on his belly to get up. By now he was a smelly mess from head to toe.

When Little Alvernon shuffled up to the house, he did not go in. But his mother knew he was at the door. She could smell him! "Go sit on the grass by the flower bed," she ordered. This occasion called for four extra pails of water from the well, the wash boiler for heating the water, and two washtubs set out in the yard. Little Alvernon was soaked and scrubbed in one tub, his soggy, smelly clothes in the other.

PEDERSEN

Little Alvernon didn't mind the bath so much as the conversation that went with it. Some of the comments heard that day were: "I ought to throw you right down on the manure pile and let you live there a couple of days!" And, "He ought to be skun alive!" And, "He sure needs his hide tanned!"

They even invented a new one. After he had been scrubbed from toenails to fingernails, someone said, "Suppose we ought to run him through the clothes wringer?"

But Little Alvernon's mother laughed, gave him a big hug after he was clean, and said, "Oh, Little Alvernon, won't you ever learn? Now, go finish your chores, and try to stay out of trouble!"

The Third Mistake

As often happened in the hen house, one of the hens stole
a nest – that is, hid her eggs.

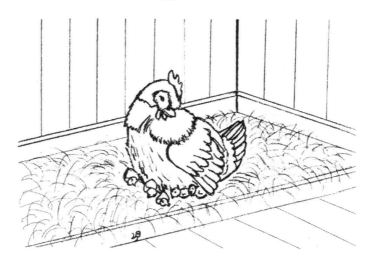

In due time she hatched a family. (Hatching happens
when the chicks peck their way out of their shells.)

As time passed, she lost all except one of her chickens by unfortunate accidents. She mothered this one chick all summer. He grew to be a red rooster larger than his mother, but she kept feeding and watching over him just the same.

Now, if a barefoot boy happened to go into the barn where the hen and her rooster son were eating, all the little boy had to do to make the rooster squawk was to reach down and make believe he was going to scoop him up. The mother hen would fly to protect her baby. Could it be that the little boy enjoyed this?

On one occasion, the conditions were right, and Little Alvernon reached down to tease the rooster. But this proved to be a big mistake. The rooster protested loudly: "SQUAWK, SQUAWK, SQUAWK!"

The mother hen fluttered her wings in preparation for battle and advanced on Little Alvernon. He always wondered how a creature with no teeth could do so much damage to a pair of bare legs.

He started for the open barn door at a dead run. Then a new adversary entered the fray. Grandma must have been in the tie-up and heard the fuss. She came through one of the little doors with a switch in her hand.

By this time, the old biddy (the hen, not Little Alvernon's grandmother) had forgotten what had started the fracas in the first place and returned to her son. But Grandma took up the chase, muttering threats like the ones Little Alvernon had heard during his bath.

Little Alvernon tore out of the big barn door as fast as he could go. Then tragedy struck. He stubbed his toe and fell flat on his stomach. But, because he was still being chased, he started crawling on all fours, scrambling down the dirt road toward Augusta.

Then the unbelievable happened. Little Alvernon heard a big THUMP. Looking back he saw that his grandmother had also fallen down and was crawling along right behind him, her switch hitting the ground at every move toward him...WHACK, WHACK, WHACK.

Little Alvernon, being more agile, recovered first. He got to his feet, and ran as fast as he could to his secret hiding place in the stable where he could peek out and see the front of the house.

As soon as his grandmother disappeared into the house, he scooted back across the road to play in the sawdust pile, unaware that his next predicament would sneak up on him on a hot Sunday afternoon in August.

© 2013

Elder Weeks

There were two places of worship in Windsor: the large Methodist Church below Windsor Corner, which was about a six-mile trip (by horse and buggy, of course) and the chapel just up the road at Tyler's Corner. The predicament in which Little Alvernon found himself happened in the little chapel. It was a beastly hot Sunday afternoon in August, and a small congregation had gathered. Although all the windows had been opened, not a whisper of a breeze stirred the air.

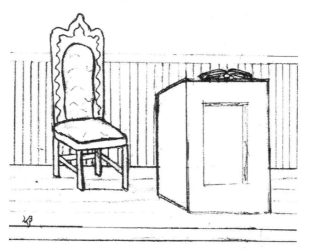

Little Alvernon had gotten special permission to sit on the platform up front. It was quite an honor to sit behind the pulpit on one of the big chairs with the fancy high backs and red cushioned seats. As part of his Sunday best clothes, he was wearing his shiny black boxed-toed shoes, which he liked to show off by putting his foot up on his knee like his father did.

It was customary for an elder to be in charge of the meeting and to preach the sermon. There were the usual parts of the service: singing of hymns, reading of scripture, important announcements, and special music. Little Alvernon especially enjoyed hearing his father sing bass in the mixed quartet with Uncle Had, Aunt Ida, and Aunt Frances. His favorite was his father's solo in "Asleep in the Deep" when his bass voice seemed to go down to the cellar on the last note. It always gave Little Alvernon a catch in his chest.

Elder Weeks had already preached once at his own church at the Mills. Now he was preaching a second time here in the chapel. He launched into his lengthy sermon, and his smooth soft voice droned on and on. Little Alvernon began to get very drowsy in the plush comfortable chair. He closed his eyes.

Perhaps he began to dream about the picnic planned for this afternoon on Three Mile Pond and the special chicken dish his mother had prepared to take along. If the evening cooled off, they would build a fire in the outdoor fireplace and gather round to sing some songs. Little Alvernon would probably fall asleep to the familiar melodies and be carried home in his father's arms.

Now it must be said that Elder Weeks was not known for being a shouting preacher, but for some reason on this occasion, perhaps to wake up his small congregation *and* himself, suddenly and without warning, POUNDED on the top of the pulpit with the flat of his hand and SHOUTED out a QUESTION!

Little Alvernon, who was now sound asleep, fell out of his chair onto the platform with a big KER-PLUNK behind Elder Weeks. He jumped to his feet, looked around at the stunned and silent congregation, stamped his little shiny black box-toed shoe on the wooden floor, and shouted,

"OH, SHOOT AND PLAGUE ON IT!"

He could feel the hot tingle of his ears turning red as he climbed back up into the high-backed, red-cushioned chair. He sat very straight and still, with his eyes looking down at his folded hands, for the rest of the sermon.

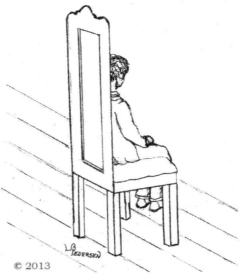

© 2013

Drop the Handkerchief

L ittle Alvernon went to school in what we would call a one-room schoolhouse where students of all ages were taught together by one teacher. Older students sometimes helped the younger ones with their lessons. The teacher's desk was up front on a platform where the big blackboard was. The students' desks were bolted to the floor in rows one behind the other. Sometimes two children shared a desk. Each student had a small blackboard and some chalk to practice writing and arithmetic.

In warm weather, the windows on each side were opened to let in cooling breezes. For heat in the cold winter months, the big black potbellied woodstove was fired up, and the older boys usually helped with hauling wood and keeping the fire going.

One fall at school, Little Alvernon found himself admiring a certain girl. You might say he had a crush on her. Her name was Flora. He never told anyone because he was shy. He was afraid the other kids would tease him. You see, Little Alvernon was small and weighed about 70 pounds. Flora was one of the bigger girls in school and was about twice his size. So he kept his secret to himself.

Sometimes when recess or lunchtime came, ten or fifteen school children formed a circle and played a game called "Drop the Handkerchief." If a girl was "IT," she dropped the cloth handkerchief behind a boy, who snatched it up and then tried to catch her before she got back to the empty place that he had left. If a boy was "IT," he dropped the handkerchief behind a girl, and the same rules applied. If the one who dropped the handkerchief got caught, he (or she) was supposed to get kissed!

On one particular day, Flora was IT, and she dropped the handkerchief behind Little Alvernon. Now, he had not thought much about what he would do if Flora chose him, but when she did, he realized his smaller size gave him an advantage. Little Alvernon could run faster than Flora. Before she got halfway around the circle, he caught her, pulled her head down and kissed her SMACK on the lips.

© 2013

In two shakes of a lamb's tail, Flora hauled off and BAM gave Little Alvernon a left jab to the eye, then POW, a hard right cross to the chin. Little Alvernon went down! He not only went down, but he turned a complete somersault, skidded three feet and landed on his back. But he did not feel bad. In fact, he felt very good. He seemed to be lying on a soft fleecy cloud, the ground whirling around him at a remarkable rate.

Little Alvernon chose to stay where he was for the time being. No one in the circle spoke. Everyone turned so that they could see what was going on. Flora stood over Little Alvernon with her hands on her hips. Little Alvernon did not move. The ground gradually stopped spinning. He was glad that he had not tried to get up and had taken this time to meditate on his situation.

Then something happened. Remember that Little Alvernon was inclined to be shy, or bashful, as some call it. A wave of red began to creep over his features – right from his heart, you might say. It crept up his neck and spread over his face all the way up to the roots of his dark brown, wavy hair. Then the sweetest smile appeared on his face. It was a wonder to see. At that particular moment, Little Alvernon was handsome. Never before had he been such a handsome young man. It was at that moment he knew for sure that Flora loved him.

The Ice Pond

Up the hill from the crossroads lived another little boy whose middle name was Ellsworth. Everyone called him Summy, although that was not his real first name. Little Alvernon was not always called by his real name either. Sometimes he was called "Bubbah," or just "Bub," a nickname that his younger brother Johnnie gave him because he could not say the word "brother." This Little Alvernon story mostly concerns Summy and Bubbah, although all the other schoolboys were there, too.

Across the road from the schoolhouse, there was a pasture that sloped down to a section of the town called the Neck. At the foot of the hill, there was a pond. It was not very large – probably as long as your driveway and just about as wide. The water was about three feet deep most of the time. Now-a-days, it might be called a farm pond. Little Alvernon and his friends called it the Ice Pond. In the warm months of the year they would get permission to go there and swim, and in the cold months, they would skate on the ice.

On this particular Thursday and Friday, the boys had been skating on the pond, because there had been a cold spell to freeze it over nicely. To understand how Little Alvernon's next predicament came about, you must know what happened with the outside temperature that weekend. The weather came off warmer on Saturday and Sunday melting the ice. But then on Sunday night, it was very cold again, and by Monday noon, when the boys returned to play, the ice on the pond looked just as it had on Friday. As the boys neared the pond, everybody was racing to be the first to slide across the ice. No one knew why Little Alvernon got there first this time, but as he made a dash to slide on the ice, instead of sliding across, he slid out of sight, with a soft CRACKLE and SPLASH.

Little Alvernon was up to his knees, then up to his waist, then almost up to his neck in the cold, icy water. He gasped and dropped his skates into the pond. He knew all the boys were shouting, but the only voice he heard was Summy's screaming, "CAN YOU GET OUT, BUBBAH? CAN YOU GET OUT?"

The bottom of the pond was slippery clay and slanted downward from the edges. After a bit of scrambling, Little Alvernon got out all right, and someone fished out his skates, but his predicament was not over by any means. There was that quarter of a mile climb up the hill to the schoolhouse, and then that long mile home from there.

As they started up the hill, another problem developed. Little Alvernon's clothing began to freeze. This made it very difficult to walk, and he began to sound like a knight in metal armor: CLINK, CLINK, CLINK with every step.

When they finally made it to the road by the schoolhouse, everyone began shouting, "WHOA! WHOA! WAIT! WAIT!"

How fortunate it was that a neighbor, Will Bean, was passing by with his horse and wagon. Will cramped the front wheels around so Little Alvernon could use the round step-up and climb into the wagon.

Even though Will wrapped him up in the wagon blankets, Little Alvernon's teeth chattered all the way home.

When Will drove into the door yard, Little Alvernon's mother came to the door to inquire what the trouble was. Little Alvernon climbed down from the wagon. As he made his way stiffly into the house. Will was already backing his horses out of the yard.

He said, "Fell in the pond," and was gone. He had chores to do and a day's work ahead of him still.

One more thing remained to be done: dig out the washtub, fill it with pails of water heated on the wood stove, and put Little Alvernon into a nice warm bath.

His mother stood his stiff, frozen long johns in the boiler behind the stove to melt.

The next time Little Alvernon went skating, you may be sure that he did a bit of testing before he slid across the Ice Pond.

The Frosty Latch

Another cold winter day set the stage for Little Alvernon's next predicament. Although it was quite frosty, the sun was shining brightly, and Little Alvernon decided that it was pleasant enough to play outdoors. He put on his handmade coat, his wool mittens, his galoshes, and his stocking cap with a tassel on the end that hung down below his waist. (This was a very special kind of hat, knitted by his grandmother, and made long enough to be wrapped around his neck and face as a scarf on cold, windy days.)

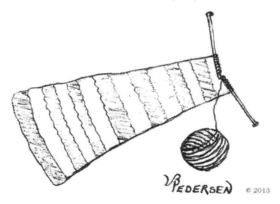

Little Alvernon took out his Flexible Flyer sled and for a time had fun sliding down the little slope just above the driveway leading to the stable. But soon he came up with another fine idea. Why not go up to the henhouse and see if there were some eggs?

Fried eggs, buttered toast, and hot chocolate sounded very good to him right at this moment. So from the top of the knoll, he trudged up the snowy path pulling his sled by the rope.

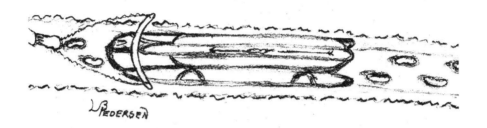

His galoshes went CRUNCH, CRUNCH, CRUNCH, and the runners of his sled went SWOOSH, SWOOSH, SWOOSH. Little Alvernon hummed a tune, keeping time with the winter sounds.

When he got to the old henhouse, some distance away from the house, he leaned his Flexible Flyer against the building.

His predicament began when he reached for the metal latch to open the henhouse door. He had heard that if you put your tongue on a piece of cold and frosty metal, it would stick right there. Could that be true?

Watch out, Little Alvernon! Experience is a tough teacher – she is apt to test first and teach afterward.

He studied the latch on the henhouse door. Leaning over a bit, he stuck out his tongue. Closer and closer he came. Then, CONTACT! UH, OH, the old saying was true! There he was, slightly bent over, with his little red tongue stuck fast to the cold frosty latch.

Now remember, this was in the country. The house was a hundred yards away, and the barn was across the road. There were no people walking on the road. There was no one nearby. This was a real predicament. Did you ever try to shout, "HELP!" without using your tongue? You see, there is the letter "L" in the word HELP, and it is quite hard to say with your tongue outside your mouth.

I'll say this for Little Alvernon, he did not panic and try to pull away. This would have ripped the skin from his tongue. He stayed put. His back began to ache from his stooped-over position, but he still did not move. He started to think he would have to stay there until spring.

All at once, he had an idea! He took off his mittens, cupped his hands around his tongue and the latch, and started to breathe in through his nose and out through his mouth. In and out ... in and out...

Steam began to rise around his face.

He kept at it, until suddenly, it happened! HIS TONGUE CAME OFF! Ohhhh! I don't mean his tongue came off and lay there flopping on the frosty latch. NO! I mean that the latch let go of his tongue, and Little Alvernon wasn't stuck anymore. Did you ever feel free? He certainly did at that very moment.

We don't know what Little Alvernon did next. But we can imagine that he lifted the latch of the hen house door with his mittened hand, went in to gather some eggs, and carried them carefully back to the house.

Perhaps he sat at the table by the big black cook stove and told his mother about his latest predicament while she cooked him a hot, tasty meal.

We DO know that Little Alvernon never forgot the lesson of the frosty latch, even when he was grown up, because he told the story over and over to his children and grandchildren, along with lots of chuckles and a twinkle in his dark brown eyes.

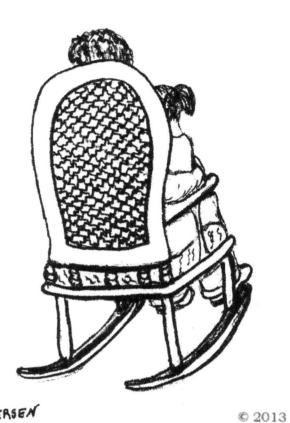

© 2013

Home built circa 1888 at Tyler's Corner
by John Williamson Boynton, Civil War Veteran

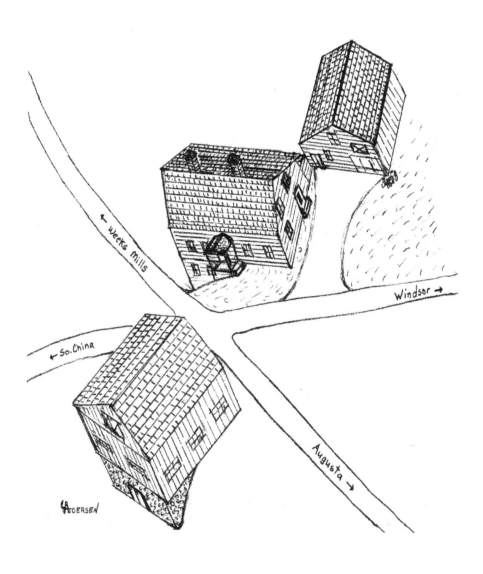

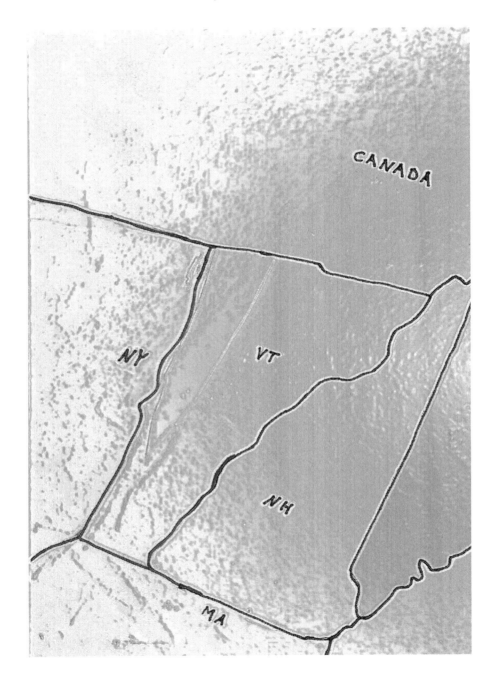

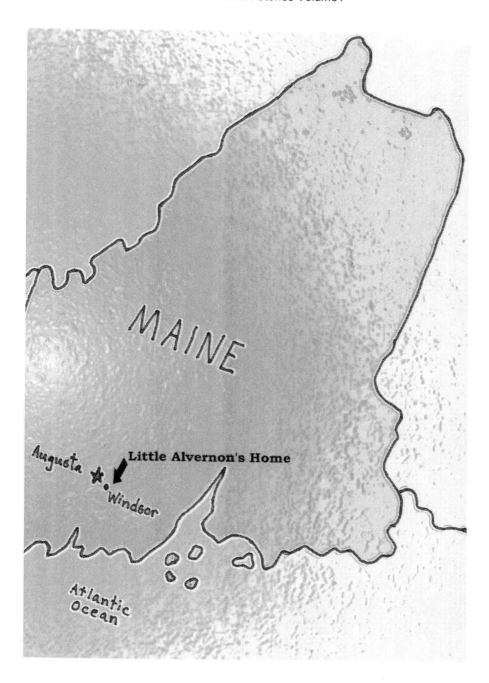

About the Author

Born of Vernon and Abbie on October 27, 1944, at the hospital in Farmington, Maine, Linda Lee Boynton was brought home to 17 Rowell Street in Madison. She slept to the sawing of wood and the pounding of nails as her parents renovated the dilapidated floors, ceilings, and walls. She was the youngest of four children and always considered the baby. She attended Weston Avenue Elementary where her mother was a kindergarten teacher and Madison Junior High where her father was the principal. Everyone knew her parents in this small mill town along the Kennebec River. It was her world until she left for college. She reminisces, "I can still see and smell the pulp that was piled high in the mill yard and hear and feel the water thundering over the dam between Madison and Anson."

Linda attended Gordon College in Wenham, Massachusetts, where she met her future husband Robert Pedersen. They were married soon after she graduated with a degree in French. Robert received an officer's commission in the army when he completed his graduate studies in counseling, and they left New England. Their first child, Cheri, was born in California. After Robert returned from duty in Vietnam, they returned to the Northeast to settle. They moved into their 1730 home in Danville, New Hampshire in 1971. Their second daughter, Jessica, and their son, Erik, were born there. Her husband began his civilian career in education.

While raising their three children in this small rural town, Linda pursued many interests and careers, including running a craft shop, designing and making gymnastic wear, and managing a department in retail. She was also involved in church activities and small group Bible studies. Much of her poetry and journal writing was done during this time. When her children were older, Linda began to consider re-instating her teacher certification.

About her decision to teach, Linda reflects, "Like many women my age who stayed home to raise a family, I entered the teaching profession later in life. I had not planned to teach. This was a surprising turn in the direction of my life. Teaching is very demanding, but I felt drawn to it – in the sense of joining my family's lineage of educators." Linda was active on the board of her state language association for twenty years. She was the editor of NHAWLT's newsletter. When she retired from full time teaching in 2008, Linda was able to concentrate on getting **The Little Alvernon Stories** published.

In 2001, Linda published a poetry anthology entitled *Words like Pebbles: the Poetic Voice of Three Generations* (ISBN 0-595-17657-7).

This compilation of poems written by women of three different generations (Linda's mother, her daughter, and herself) is amazingly similar in its inter-generational roots to the **Little Alvernon** project – reaching back in time for a clearer view of the present and an enduring hope for the future.

Watch for

The Little Alvernon Stories Volume 2

and more predicaments concerning Bessie the milk cow, getting lost in the woods, a screaming frog, a flying carpet, a tire blowout, messy cats, and a neighborhood fire...

Visit The Little Alvernon Stories website:

www.facebook.com/TheLittleAlvernonStories

Made in the USA
Charleston, SC
04 November 2013